Kobee Manatee®

Climate Change and The Great Blue Hole Hazard

Written by **Robert Scott Thayer**

Illustrated by **Lauren Gallegos**

Thompson Mill Press

For Rick and Linda -R.S.T.
For Kirsti and her family -L.G.

Visit Kobee Manatee® on the Web!
KobeeManatee.com

Many thanks go out to all who helped in the making of this book, in particular; Susan Korman, editor and Dr. Tracy Fanara,
Inspector Planet & NOAA Coastal Portfolio Modeling Manager
Published by Thompson Mill Press LLC
thompsonmillpress.com

Library of Congress Cataloging in Publication Data
Thayer, Robert Scott
Kobee manatee: climate change and the great blue hole hazard / written by Robert Scott Thayer; Illustrated by
Lauren Gallegos. – 1st ed.
p. cm.

Library of Congress Control Number: 2020913201

Summary: Kobee Manatee and his seafaring pals travel from the Grand Caymans to Belize to help Kobee's cousin Quinn with her new café, but one of the friends unfortunately plunges into the Great Blue Hole.

ISBN 978-0-9971239-9-9 (hardcover)   ISBN 978-0-9971239-5-1 (eBook)

Printed and Bound in the USA

First edition, first printing
Designed by Lauren Gallegos

Kobee's Fun Facts

The country of Belize is located on the coast of Central America. Central America is an isthmus, a narrow strip of land in the sea, that connects two bigger landmasses. This isthmus of Central America connects North America and South America.

Oh, the fun we had in Grand Cayman with those stingrays!

Now my friends and I were ready for another adventure. This time we were going to Belize to help my cousin Quinn clean up plastic litter around her new Seagrass Café.

"How far away is Belize?" Tess asked.

"About five hundred miles from the Cayman Islands," I replied.

"How long will it take us to swim there?" Pablo asked.

Kobee's Fun Facts

The Great Blue Hole in Belize lies near the center of Lighthouse Reef, about 43 miles from the mainland. The hole is part of the Belize Barrier Reef Reserve System, a World Heritage Site of the United Nations Educational, Scientific and Cultural Organization (UNESCO). The Great Blue Hole is shaped like a circle. It's about 1,000 feet across and 410 feet deep.

"Hmm …" I thought for a second. "Moving five miles per hour with some stops, it will take us about five days."

"What's in Belize?"

"It has one of the most amazing places on earth – the Great Blue Hole." I said.

Pablo laughed. "Blue hole, blue sky, everything's … b-l-u-e."

Tess and I chuckled too!

Soon we saw someone in trouble – a giant turtle struggling with plastic wrapped around its head. The turtle bobbed and tried to speak, but the plastic was too tight!
"We'll help you," I said.

Kobee's Fun Facts

Research has shown that plastic impacts nearly 700 ocean species, from the tiniest plankton to the largest whales. According to the Ocean Conservancy, nearly 8 million metric tons of plastic are dumped in our ocean every year.

Pablo bounced off me. The turtle froze as Pablo used his claws to snip the plastic.

Kobee's Fun Facts

More than fifty percent of all sea turtles consume some form of plastic during their lifetimes. After it's thrown away, plastic stays in the environment, breaking down to small particles, called microplastics. The microplastics look like plankton, but unlike plankton, they are harmful to sea life.

"Success!" Pablo called as he made the final cut.

Kobee's Fun Facts

Here's how you can be part of the fight against plastic litter:

1. *Encourage your family to bring reusable shopping bags to stores, and avoid using single-use plastic bags.*
2. *Use reusable straws made of stainless steel, glass, or bamboo instead of plastic ones.*
3. *Bring a stainless steel water bottle to school instead of plastic water bottles.*
4. *Encourage family members to wear clothing made from earth-friendly materials such as cotton and linen instead of microfibers and other synthetic fibers.*
5. *As a family or class project, return single-use bags to grocery stores for recycling.*

Kobee's Fun Facts

Shoppers in the United States use about one plastic bag per resident per day. Meanwhile, shoppers in Denmark use an average of four plastic bags a year.

"Thanks for freeing me," said the turtle. "I thought the plastic was a yummy jellyfish snack, so I swam toward it. That was a big mistake!"

"I'm glad you're safe," Tess said. "What's your name?"

"Tameeka."

"We're swimming to Belize to help my cousin Quinn with her new Seagrass Café," I said to Tameeka. "We'll help clean up some plastic litter that's on her property. Then we'll have some fun. Come along, I know you'll enjoy it!"

"Sure!" said Tameeka.

Kobee's Fun Facts

About half of all the plastic ever manufactured has been made since the year 2000. And all of the plastic ever created, is still in our environment.

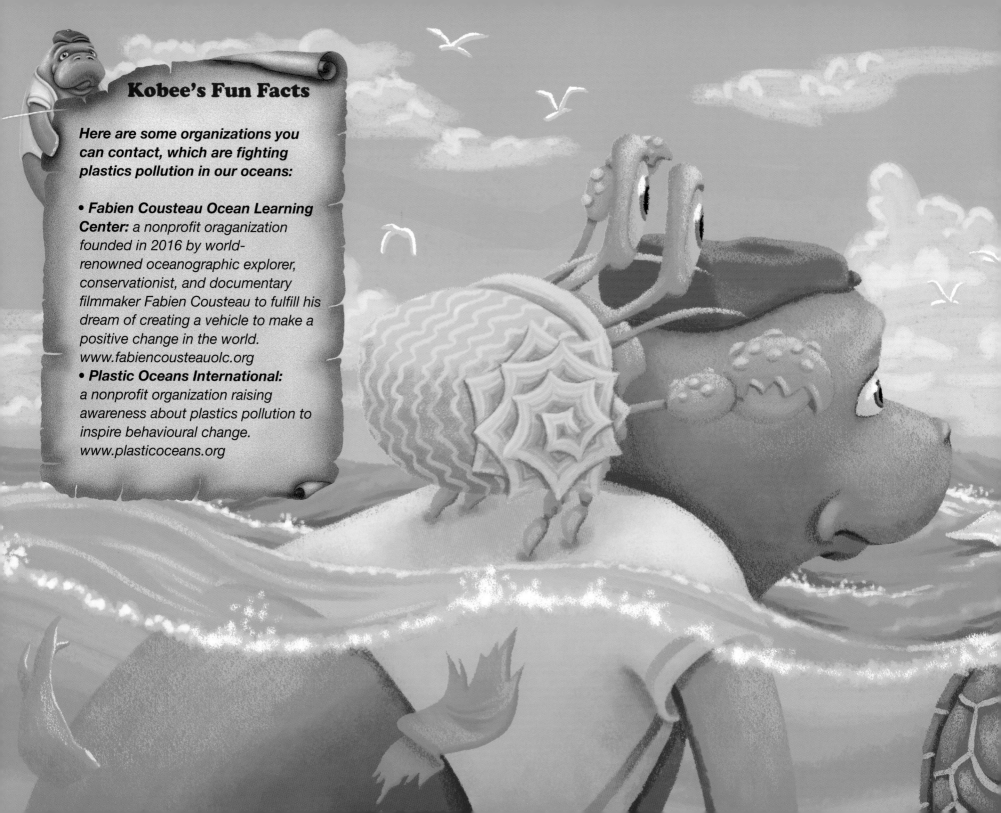

Kobee's Fun Facts

Here are some organizations you can contact, which are fighting plastics pollution in our oceans:

• *Fabien Cousteau Ocean Learning Center:* *a nonprofit oraganization founded in 2016 by world-renowned oceanographic explorer, conservationist, and documentary filmmaker Fabien Cousteau to fulfill his dream of creating a vehicle to make a positive change in the world. www.fabiencousteauolc.org*
• *Plastic Oceans International:* *a nonprofit organization raising awareness about plastics pollution to inspire behavioural change. www.plasticoceans.org*

We swam through crystal clear water and beautiful coral. Along the way, we also spotted ugly plastic trash.

"It's so colorful here, yet so sad. Humans need to stop polluting the ocean with plastic!" Tess said.

The rest of us nodded. It was upsetting to see all the garbage in the ocean.

Soon I surfaced for air, and Pablo called, "Skipper! Sailboat straight ahead!"

I gulped. "That's not a sailboat. It's a Portuguese man-of-war!"

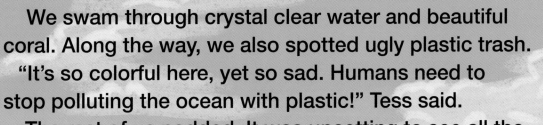

Kobee's Fun Facts

Many people mistake the Portuguese man-of-war for a jellyfish, but it's neither a fish nor a jelly! Each man-of-war is actually a whole colony of several small individual organisms. The organisms are so closely intertwined that they cannot survive alone.

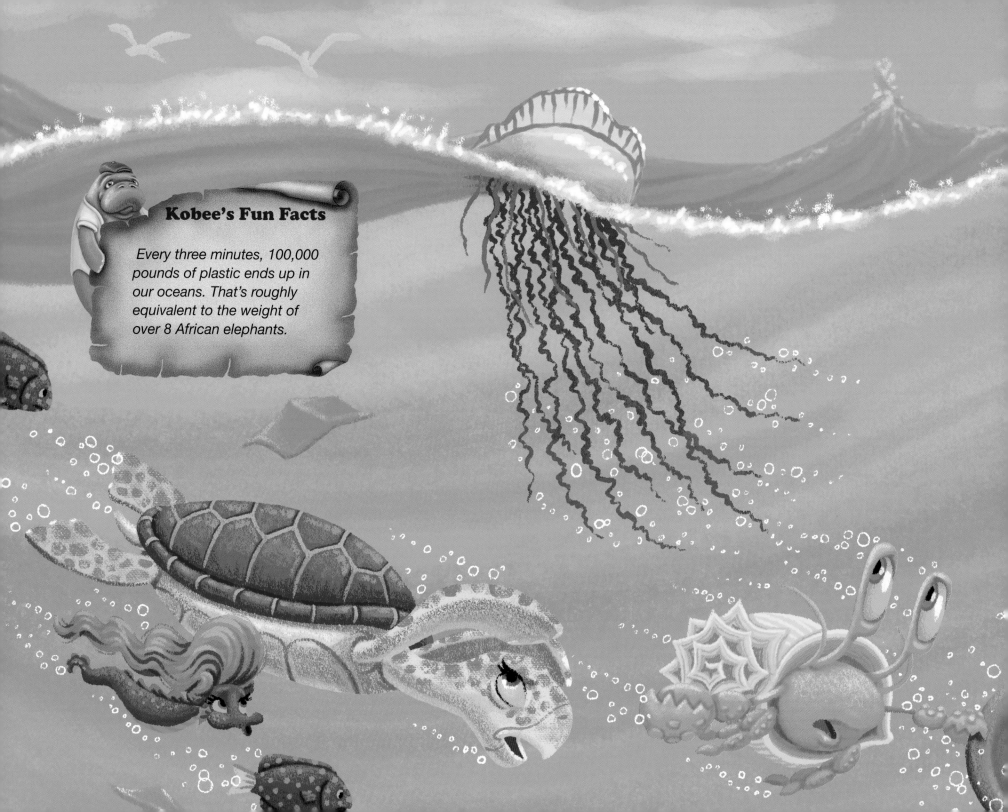

Kobee's Fun Facts

Every three minutes, 100,000 pounds of plastic ends up in our oceans. That's roughly equivalent to the weight of over 8 African elephants.

"Huh?" Pablo said. "Did you say 'war'? I don't see any fighting."

"Man-of-wars are organisms shaped like eighteenth-century Portuguese warships. They are very venomous!" I explained.

Whoosh! Without warning, the man-of-war's whip-like tentacles shot toward us.

"Tameeka, duck!" Tess cried.

Kobee's Fun Facts

Here are more organizations you can contact, which are fighting plastics pollution in our oceans:

• **5 Gyres:** *in 2009 Anna and Marcus Erikson founded the nonprofit 5 Gyres Institute to investigate key questions about plastic pollution.*
www.5gyres.org

• **Algalita:** *is a nonprofit organization founded in 1994 by Captain Charles Moore, who is credited with discovering the Great Pacific Garbage Patch. They developed the world's first set of research protocols - a.k.a. Standard Operating Procedures, or SOPs - for sampling ocean plastic pollution. Algalita's mission is research, education, and reform.*
www.algalita.org

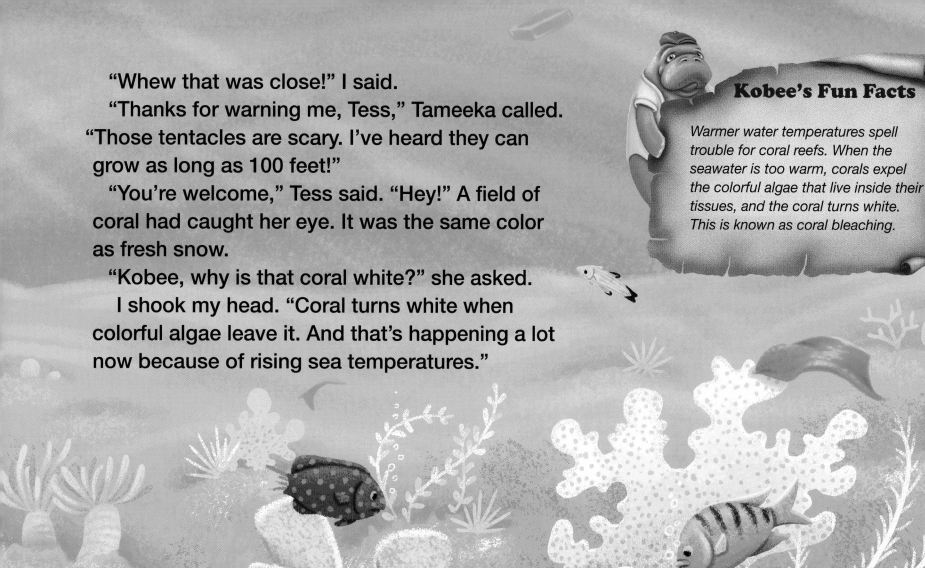

"Whew that was close!" I said.

"Thanks for warning me, Tess," Tameeka called. "Those tentacles are scary. I've heard they can grow as long as 100 feet!"

"You're welcome," Tess said. "Hey!" A field of coral had caught her eye. It was the same color as fresh snow.

"Kobee, why is that coral white?" she asked.

I shook my head. "Coral turns white when colorful algae leave it. And that's happening a lot now because of rising sea temperatures."

Kobee's Fun Facts

Warmer water temperatures spell trouble for coral reefs. When the seawater is too warm, corals expel the colorful algae that live inside their tissues, and the coral turns white. This is known as coral bleaching.

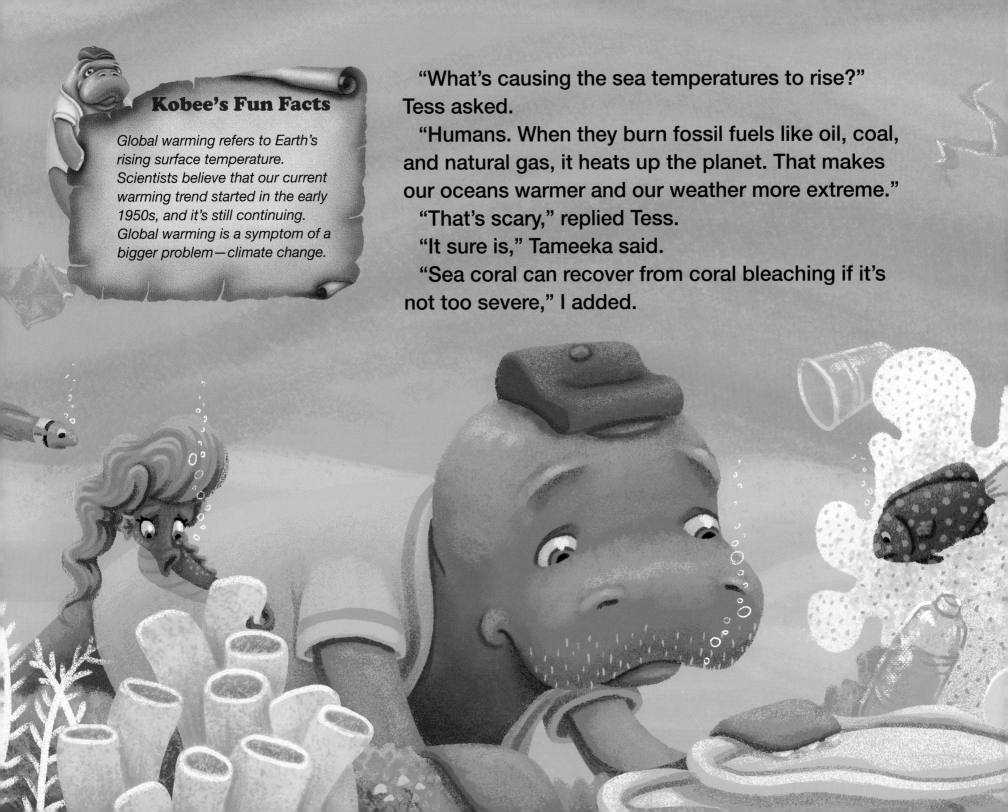

Kobee's Fun Facts

Global warming refers to Earth's rising surface temperature. Scientists believe that our current warming trend started in the early 1950s, and it's still continuing. Global warming is a symptom of a bigger problem—climate change.

"What's causing the sea temperatures to rise?" Tess asked.

"Humans. When they burn fossil fuels like oil, coal, and natural gas, it heats up the planet. That makes our oceans warmer and our weather more extreme."

"That's scary," replied Tess.

"It sure is," Tameeka said.

"Sea coral can recover from coral bleaching if it's not too severe," I added.

"Humans need to stop doing things that cause climate change," grumbled Pablo. "Yes," I agreed. "Humans can help our oceans and environment by using fewer plastics and fossil fuels."

Kobee's Fun Facts

Climate change has been caused by people's burning of fossil fuels (coal, oil, and natural gas) for cars, manufacturing, and to warm and cool our homes and schools. The burning of fossil fuels releases greenhouse gases (carbon dioxide, methane, nitrous oxide and ozone) into the atmosphere. The gases trap heat, which changes our weather and warms our oceans. Now for the good news – humans caused climate change, so they have the tools for solving the problem too!

We kept swimming toward Belize. One afternoon Tess wobbled off me to gobble some shrimp. Suddenly a spotted scorpionfish leaped out at her! I swooped down and saved Tess just in time.

"Yikes! Thanks, Kobee," Tess said. "That fish was camouflaged among the rocks. I didn't see it."

"Like Portuguese man-of-wars, scorpionfish are venomous," I said.

"I'm glad you're—Ahh!" Just ahead, I saw a dark blue monster, which grew bigger… and … B-I-G-G-E-R.

Kobee's Fun Facts

Every day, people around the world use 12 million barrels of oil to make plastic. That's equivalent to the weight of 1,800,000 medium-sized cars! Plastic now makes up ninety percent of all trash floating on the ocean surface.

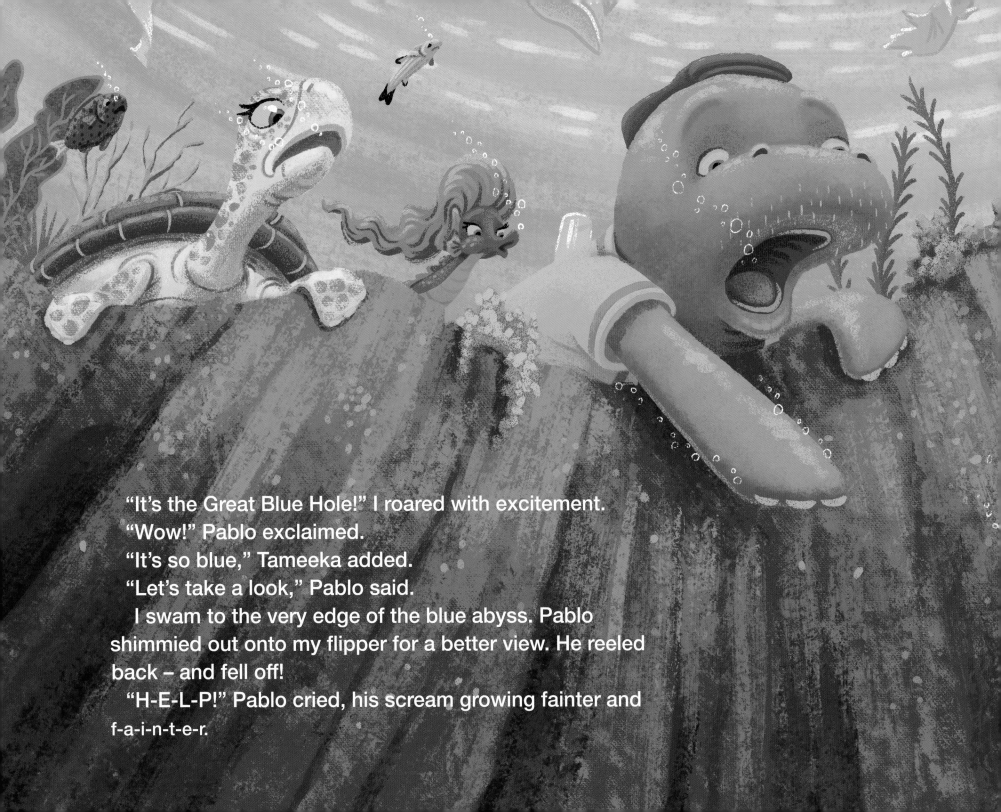

"It's the Great Blue Hole!" I roared with excitement.

"Wow!" Pablo exclaimed.

"It's so blue," Tameeka added.

"Let's take a look," Pablo said.

I swam to the very edge of the blue abyss. Pablo shimmied out onto my flipper for a better view. He reeled back – and fell off!

"H-E-L-P!" Pablo cried, his scream growing fainter and f-a-i-n-t-e-r.

Kobee's Fun Facts

The Great Blue Hole formed as a limestone cave hundreds of thousands of years ago, when sea levels were very low. At the end of the last ice age, sea levels rose by around 300 feet, and water filled the cave. The site became famous in 1971 when Jacques Cousteau explored it. He declared it one of the top five scuba-diving sites in the world because of its depth and beauty.

"Here we come, Pablo!" I shouted.
Tess was terrified as I began the descent into the giant hole. But Tameeka swiftly dove past me.

Kobee's Fun Facts

Giant stalactites, which look like huge hanging icicles can be found inside the Great Blue Hole. Scientists believe these were formed in a dry cavern above sea level during glacial periods.

Tameeka paddled rapidly, sinking deeper and deeper until I couldn't see her anymore. I felt scared as I dove down. I couldn't find anything. I was very worried about Pablo. Would he make it back safe? Then all at once, something appeared, rising from the Great Blue Hole.

"It's Tameeka and Pablo!" Tess called.
"Welcome back," I cried with relief.
Pablo stumbled back onboard.
"I dove quickly, as Pablo went into a downward spiral," Tameeka said.

Kobee's Fun Facts

The first explorations of the Great Blue Hole were made by ocean pioneer and diver Jacques-Yves Cousteau. He and his team from the ship Calypso charted the depth of the hole in 1971. Then in 2018 Cousteau's oldest grandson, Fabien Cousteau, returned to the Great Blue Hole with Sir Richard Branson and another team of explorers.

Pablo quivered. "Thanks, Tameeka – that was scary."

"You're welcome," Tameeka said.

"Hooray Pablo's safe!" Tess exclaimed.

Kobee's Fun Facts

The Great Blue Hole is so deep that sunlight cannot reach its depths, and plants and plankton can't survive. You can dive there, but the best way to see the hole's amazing beauty is from a plane or helicopter.

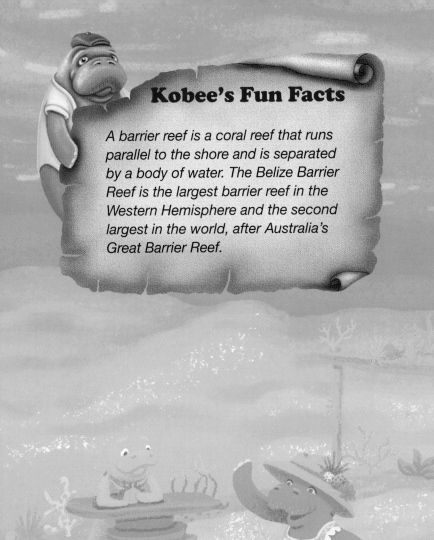

Kobee's Fun Facts

A barrier reef is a coral reef that runs parallel to the shore and is separated by a body of water. The Belize Barrier Reef is the largest barrier reef in the Western Hemisphere and the second largest in the world, after Australia's Great Barrier Reef.

"Kobee, will we meet Quinn soon?" asked Pablo.

"Very soon," I replied. I swam over the awesome Belize barrier reef.

"There's the cafe!" Tameeka said.

Pablo grinned. "Such a cool-looking place. All the manatees are eating seagrass subs."

"K-O-B-E-E!" I heard a sweet voice—a cheerful manatee was waving at me.

"Quinn!" I called. "It's great seeing you, cuz!"
"Great seeing you too, Kobee," she replied.
"Ready to try my seagrass specialty?"
"Sure," I said.

"Before we eat, I need your help cleaning up some plastic litter around here," Quinn said. "I know it's a lot of work, but once we're done – we'll have plenty of fun!"

Kobee's Fun Facts

The Great Pacific Garbage Patch is a mass of litter floating in the north Pacific Ocean. It is a huge patch of debris, twice the size of Texas. Because of its Pacific Ocean location, between the U.S. and Japan, cleaning it up is no one nation's responsibility.

Kobee's Fun Facts

In 2019 a United Nations report warned that sea levels were rising much faster than originally forecast. Due to climate change, glaciers and ice sheets from Greenland to Antarctica are quickly melting.

Then after the plastic litter was gone, everyone celebrated. I grabbed a guitar and sang about our Great Blue Hole adventure!

Kobee's Fun Facts

Here are some more important organizations you can contact, which are fighting plastics pollution in our oceans:

- **Oceana:** the largest organization in the world devoted to marine conservation. www.oceana.org
- **4Ocean:** a global movement for removing plastic litter from our oceans and coastlines. www.4ocean.com/about
- **The Ocean Conservancy:** works with millions of volunteers of all ages, as part of their International Coastal Cleanup. www.oceanconservancy.org
- **The Plastic Pollution Coalition:** a growing global alliance of individuals, organizations, and businesses working toward a world free of plastics pollution. www.plasticpollutioncoalition.org